FAIRY FOREST

Mary M. Cushnie-Mansour

CAVERN
OF DREAMS
PUBLISHING

D1637916

Mary M. Cushnie-Mansour is a master fantasy story-teller, and Fairy Forest is a beautifully wrapped gift to readers young and old. In a delightfully musical and gently lilting style, Cushnie-Mansour weaves together a magical adventure featuring fairies, elves, ravens, wolves, banshees, and humans, all while showcasing the strength, humour, and resilience of her young, female heroine, Kalani.

R. Jetleb,
Author of the
"What About" and "Mall Girl" series.

Books by Mary M. Cushnie-Mansour

Youth Novels
A Story of Day & Night
The Silver Tree
Fairy Forest

Children's Picture Books
The Official Tickler
The Seahorse and the Little Girl With Big Blue Eyes
Curtis the Crock
Dragon Disarray
The Old Woman of the Mountain
Bedtime Stories

Bilingual Children's Books (English/French)
Teensy Weensy Spider
Alexandra's Christmas Surprise
Charlie Seal Meets a Fairy Seal
Charlie and the Elves
Curtis the Crock
Freddy Frog's Frolic
The Day Bo Found His Bark
Jesse's Secret
The Temper Tantrum

Short Stories
From the Heart
Mysteries From the Keys

Poetry
picking up the pieces
Life's Rollercoaster
Devastations of Mankind
Shattered
Memories

Detective Toby Mysteries
Are You Listening to Me?
Running Away From Loneliness
Past Ghosts
Saving Alora

Night's Vampire Series
Night's Gift
Night's Children
Night's Return
Night's Temptress
Night's Betrayals
Night's Revelations
Night's Rescue

Biography
A 20th Century Portia

Fairy Forest

Ordering Information:
Books can be ordered directly from the author's website: http://www.writerontherun.ca or through Amazon (direct links are on author's website) For volume order discounts, contact the author via email, mary@writerontherun.ca

Artwork by Jennifer Bettio

CAVERN OF DREAMS PUBLISHING
Brantford, ON, Canada

Available on Amazon in print and Ebook formats

ISBN 9798666916186

Every time a child says, "I don't believe in fairies," there is a fairy somewhere that falls down dead.
~James Matthew Barrie, Peter Pan

Dedicated to those who still believe in fairies and in the conservation of the beautiful, sacred "Fairy Forest!"

Fairies are invisible and inaudible like angels. But their magic sparkles in nature.
~Lynn Holland

Prologue

The Irish have always believed in fairies, and in protecting the forests' nymphs. There is one forest in particular, deep in the heart of Ireland, sacred to the people who still believe. It is called "Fairy Forest."

Many centuries ago, there was a time-honoured pact established between humans and fairies. As civilization expanded, humankind began encroaching on forests where fairies roamed freely, driving them from their homes. The fairies finally took refuge in a vast tract of forest in the heart of Ireland, building their new home beneath the roots of the ancient trees.

Eventually, the fairies were joined by Elves, who made their homes in the branches of the trees, and the two kingdoms allied. After much deliberation, the fairies and elves decided to approach the humans and strike a deal.

This all took place at a time when men and fairies and elves still gathered together and broke bread and drank wine. So it was, the fairies and elves went to the humans in the town that had jurisdiction over Fairy Forest and asked for protection of the woodland.

Fortunately, the men in the town wanted to protect their magical friends, for they well remembered the pages in the history books about how fairies and elves had fought with humans during the great wars when horrendous forces of inhuman creatures had tried to conquer the land. Papers were drawn up, protecting Fairy Forest. It was written on the pages that no human would set foot inside the forest to destroy any part of it. It would forever be a sanctuary for the fairies and elves.

Papers were signed, and it was agreed upon that a wall would also be built around Fairy Forest to keep out those tempted to enter, especially those who would come after and did not know of the historic agreement. The fairies, elves, and humans built the wall together, from the stones of the fields. The final paragraph in the document stated the treaty was good for as long as there was even one fairy or elf alive, and for as long as the surrounding towns had at least one human living in them.

So it was written, and so Fairy Forest remained, untouched - until now.

Chapter One

Kalani raced through the hallways of the underground fairy fortress. She knew the well-trodden route perfectly, having lived there her entire life. The young fairy's dark curls bounced with each step she took, and Kalani's eyes flamed red as she went over in her mind the story she was about to relay to her mother.

"Someone has destroyed a section of the stone fence surrounding our forest!" Kalani informed, bursting into her mother's chambers.

"How do you know this, daughter?" Shanaye questioned.

Shanaye was one of the most beautiful fairies in the forest. Her features were petite, her skin smooth. Her hair shimmered like silver as it flowed down her back, sweeping the tips of her ankles. Shanaye always wore a smile, and the wisdom of ages shone from her eyes, for she was born in a time when fairies were not confined to one area, when they were able to roam the hills and valleys of Ireland at will, from the north to the south, the east to the west.

"The twins, Gavin and Gavina, informed me," Kalani replied.

"From where was this information gathered?" Shanaye tilted her head questioningly.

"The twins observed it as they flew through the forest. They were exploring the far side of the woodland and suddenly found themselves being chased by some men who had come upon them in a huge machine with wheels. Gavin and Gavina had to transform into their hawk forms so they could escape."

"Why were they being chased?" Shanaye was curious.

"Gavina told me that she and her brother were down by the river that runs at the edge of our forest, inside the wall, and they discovered some big machines sitting outside the opening of the broken wall - the twins were playing on them when these men drove up. There was a loud blasting sound Gavina said, like the horn we blow to open our festivities, but not as pleasant to the ears. Their machine stopped, and there was a great cloud of dust all around it. When the dust settled, the men were running toward Gavina and Gavin, shouting and looking very angry. The twins decided it would be better to get out of there!"

"At what point did they change?" Shanaye was concerned. If the children were scared and transformed before they were out of sight of those men, it might not bode well for the fairies.

"Gavin said they waited until they were under cover of the forest before changing into hawks. He was laughing as he told me how they watched the men from the high branches of the trees. He said the men looked so confused, and one of them yelled, 'how did those little...' I cannot use such a word as Gavin did, Mother, 'get away!'"

"Did Gavin and Gavina notice anything else out of place?" Shanaye inquired, a note of worry in her voice.

"Yes, they said some of our fairy stones were moved."

"Where did the twins notice this?"

"They were flying back to the portal and spotted a rough pathway that had not been there before, and as they were chanting the opening song, Gavina detected two stones out of place. They were turned on their sides." Kalani stared at her mother, her own eyes bright with importance.

"We must bring this before King Ailbhe. Where are Gavina and Gavin now?"

"In their rooms."

"Fetch them; this story must be relayed in their own words to the King."

Kalani went off to do her mother's bidding. Shanaye paced. It was beginning again. It had been years since they were disturbed - 99 to be exact. During the last attempted destruction, her son, Ivor, was killed. When Kalani was born, the girl child had only taken away some of the pain; Shanaye did not think she could bear the loss of another child. She left her room and made her way to the King's chambers. Her daughter and the twins were waiting outside the door. She told the guard she had something of utmost importance to relay to the King, and their entrance was granted.

Chapter Two

"Where did those kids go?" the tallest of the three men looked around, confused.

"I have no idea, Néall."

"Did you see where?" Néall turned to the third man.

"No, I'm as baffled as you guys. We better tell Killian, especially if they were some local kids from the villages around here. Killian said we had to keep our project quiet until it was too late for anyone to do anything about it."

"You got that right," Néall commented. "That's the reason he had us start on this side of the forest - no towns in sight of here."

Néall and his two co-workers, Liam and Conor, headed back to their truck. Néall had an uncomfortable feeling about this project, knowing the locals were very superstitious. There was a rumour this was a protected forest and that fairies lived beneath the forest floor. Stories circulated of the doom that would reign down on anyone who disturbed them. Néall did not actually believe in fairies, but he grew up in a small town and was only too aware of how superstitions could become realities in the minds of the townspeople - especially the older ones who still dwelt on the old tales.

"Which one of us should tell Killian?" Liam mumbled.

Conor turned his face and looked out the truck window. Néall drummed his fingers on the steering wheel. "I'll do it," he growled, realizing the other two wouldn't step up to the plate. After all, he was the foreman.

Chapter Three

King Ailbhe stroked his beard thoughtfully. Age was creeping on him, and he knew that soon the throne would have to be passed on to another. The news Gavin and Gavina brought was disturbing. Ailbhe had been King for 500 years and had experienced many endeavours from outsiders to destroy the Fairy Forest. The last challenge almost ended in disaster, but Elves had come to the rescue and the evil forces - the humans - had been driven back. A deal was struck with nearby townspeople, agreeing to allow no cutting of trees or development on any land within a ten-mile range of the stone fence that surrounded the forest. Either the townspeople had a change of heart or knew nothing of what was happening.

The King summoned Rowan to his chambers. Rowan had been a faithful advisor to more than one King over the centuries. His birth was the result of a spiritual union between a fairy princess and an elf prince. No one knew exactly how old he was. Rowan's hair was as white as the snow on the distant mountain tops, his eyes as blue as the glaciers, his skin brown from the sun. He was wispy-thin, but his arm muscles rippled with strength.

Ailbhe explained the situation. "I need you to attend the next town council meeting to see if this is an outsider or if the townspeople have forgotten their promise to us. Also, before you leave, please send a message to King Fintan, informing the elves of these happenings. I feel in my bones we might be in for some trouble!"

"Yes, your Majesty," Rowan bowed, turned, and left.

Chapter Four

Killian's brow furrowed in anger. "How could you let them escape? Do you realize the amount of money I've invested in this project and the people I've dealt with to get that money?" Killian bellowed, his face becoming more crimson by the second. "Do you realize what these people will do to me - to us - if this project does not go through?"

Conor and Liam looked down at the floor. Néall faced his boss. "They just disappeared into thin air. We entered the woods seconds behind them and could see no sign of anyone."

"Just a couple birds flapping around up in a tree," Liam managed to stutter.

"Are you sure it wasn't a couple of children clapping in glee because they'd given you lot the slip, and you were too worse for the drink to notice?" Killian commented sarcastically. Liam blushed in embarrassment.

"We were not worse for the drink, Killian; the children just disappeared," Néall stated emphatically.

"I suppose next you are going to be telling me they were actually little fairies!" Killian snorted.

"I wouldn't even suggest that," Néall answered. "I do have a proposal though; one of us should go to the next town council meeting and see if they have wind of anything. We moved in big equipment, and even though we did so under the cloak of darkness, who knows if someone noticed."

"Maybe the fairies saw you!" Killian said mockingly, still playing on the fairy theme. He paused. "Well, I would suggest you be the one to attend this meeting, Néall; these other two would be useless at gaining information. Their eyes would be glued to the floor the entire time, I am sure!"

Néall nodded. "Yes, sir."

"In the meantime, I would suggest you move the equipment just inside the edge of the forest in case any prying eyes are around. Get it done tonight after dark." Killian paused. "Pile the stones back up so at least from a distance no one will be able to tell we're taking the forest down," he added. "Do whatever else you have to do to ensure the concealment of our project." Killian began walking away. "Report back to me after the meeting, Néall, which, by the way, is when?" he called back without turning around.

"Tomorrow night," Néall replied.

Chapter Five

Kalani, Gavin, and Gavina sat around a corner table in the main hall. Gavin was excited. "You need to see those machines!"

"The King would not be pleased if we were to venture out," Kalani said. "He gave strict orders that no children were to venture to the surface until the elders discover what is going on."

"No one will see us in the dark," Gavin smirked. "Are you two in or not?"

The girls looked at each other. Finally, they nodded their heads. "We're in," Gavina affirmed. "We cannot allow you to venture on your own, as careless as you are," she smiled mischievously at her twin.

"Good, we meet back here after evening vespers," Gavin grinned, happy he'd have company for his adventure.

Kalani made her way to her quarters, feeling apprehensive about what she had agreed to do. Gavin and Gavina were her best friends, but Gavin was a handful most times. The twins' parents died ten years ago when they mistakenly ate some poison berries. They had flown out of the forest and miscalculated the distance they were from their home. Hunger began to gnaw at their bellies, and seeing a bush laden with red berries, the twins' father began pecking at the luscious fruit, their mother following suit. They barely made it back to Fairy Forest.

After the funeral, Kalani's mother had taken charge of the twins as much as she was able. Gavina and Kalani became best friends, trying their best to keep Gavin from pursuing too much mischief.

Kalani lay on her bed and closed her eyes. *Maybe I'll sleep and miss the rendezvous ... then I won't get in trouble.* Kalani could only hope that was how it would turn out, but she knew better. She knew her body would wake her at the designated time and she would have to help Gavina control her wayward brother.

Chapter Six

Conor and Liam were cursing the day they had taken the job with Killian, but they'd had no choice - jobs were scarce. Unlike Néall, who didn't believe in fairies, Conor and Liam did. They'd heard too many stories of fairy sightings and of what fays would do to humans should the humans *tick them off!*

The clearing was almost ready. It would be just big enough for the two machines, and they would be able to cover the equipment with the branches from the trees they'd felled. They peered around nervously. Many of the tragic stories they'd heard took place in this forest.

"What was that?" Liam asked nervously.

Conor had heard it too. It sounded like giggling. But then again, maybe it was just the rustling of the leaves. "Probably nothin'," Conor replied as the motor from one of the machines roared to a start.

Néall drove the first piece of equipment into the clearing. While Conor and Liam covered it, he went back for the other one. Both machines inside the wall and covered, the men turned to begin restacking the rocks before leaving. A snapping sound, followed by a thud, and then a cry reached their ears. Néall leapt quickly toward the sound; Conor and Liam stood frozen.

"Tis the fairies," Liam breathed.

"Aye, it must be," Conor confirmed.

Néall returned with a young woman. She was straining against his grip. "Look what I found, gentlemen!"

Conor and Liam crossed themselves. "Tis a fairy," they breathed simultaneously.

The trees above rustled. The men looked up just as two hawks swooped down upon them.

Chapter Seven

Shanaye was worried, not having seen Kalani or the twins since supper. Something was up. Shanaye departed her chambers and proceeded to the main hall. Maybe the young ones were there playing games, but the room was empty except for Tanai and Orlaith, King Ailbhe's daughters.

"Have you seen Kalani?" Shanaye asked.

Tanai looked up. "An hour past ... she was with the twins."

"They looked to be conspiring," Orlaith added thoughtfully. "At least Gavin was - he is always up to something!"

Shanaye turned and left. Fear curdled her stomach. "Please, my lady, watch where you are going," a gentle voice bumped into her. She looked up; Rowan was gazing down at her, his soft brown eyes questioning. "Why is the lady so distracted?"

"I am in need of your advice, Rowan," Shanaye hooked her arm in his. "Is there somewhere we can go and speak privately?"

"My chambers," Rowan said, leading the way. Once inside and seated, he waited for her to speak.

"I fear my daughter and the twins may be in trouble." When Rowan said nothing, Shanaye continued. "The twins saw something today, something we told the King about."

Rowan nodded knowingly.

"I am afraid, knowing Gavin as I do, the three of them may have snuck out against the King's orders. The girls would go along with him because he would convince them with his smiles and his talk of great adventures!" Shanaye finished. Her voice shook, and Rowan wondered if it was from fear or anger.

"I am aware of what is happening," Rowan began, "The King filled me in. I am leaving tonight to inform King Fintan of the situation personally, and then I am off to attend a town council meeting tomorrow night." Rowan paused. "As for the children, my lady, do not fret so much; I am sure they have not put themselves in harm's way and will show up with a perfectly good explanation." He stood. "I must be going now."

Shanaye took the hint and made her way out of Rowan's room. He watched her go, his eyes lingering on her back for longer than necessary. His love for the beautiful fairy hidden in his heart, never to be revealed.

Chapter Eight

The hawks attacked Néall, forcing him to let go of Kalani. She tried to scuttle away but Colin and Liam, finally gathering a semblance of courage, grabbed hold of her. The birds turned on them, attacking ferociously! Néall recovered from his attack, grabbed a loose branch, and swung at the birds.

"Fly, my friends!" Kalani screamed out. "Seek Fionuir - she will help!"

Gavin and Gavina flew up into the trees.

"I'll stay with Kalani," Gavin said, "You must go and fetch the white ghost fairy - the banshee. I'll leave signs on the trail for you to follow to where these men are taking Kalani." Gavin noticed the men getting into their machine outside the wall. "Hurry, Gavina. There's no time to waste.

Gavina flew off, knowing exactly where she would find Fionuir.

Chapter Nine

King Fintan was troubled by the news. The elves, like the fairies, had led a relatively obscure life over the past 99 years. The fairies lived beneath the forest floor, the elves in the uppermost branches of the highest trees of the 500-acre forest. It was a 500-acre forest the two cultures shared. To think that humans were breaking their word and might want to take it over for development was preposterous!

"I shall gather my war council and we will meet with King Ailbhe tomorrow night. When you return from the town council meeting, we will know if we are dealing with the people we trusted or with a new adversary!"

Rowan turned and left the elf king's quarters. King Fintan watched the fairy/elf leave, then began to prepare for his trip to King Ailbhe's realm beneath the forest floor.

Chapter Ten

"What's your name, girl?" Néall growled. His left arm still pained from where the hawk's claws had grabbed at him.

Kalani remained silent. She was sitting in a dimly lit, sparsely furnished room. She had no intention of letting these men know what she was, despite two of them already thinking she was a fairy. Nor would she display her special powers - not yet - not until a need presented itself. And when Kalani started using those powers, she knew there were at least two men in the room who would tremble in fear. Kalani chuckled to herself and slumped in the chair, wanting her captors to think she was going to be easy to manipulate.

"What are we gonna do with her?" Liam whined. "We can't tell Killian; he won't like this complication!"

"Colin, grab that rope and the duct tape from over there. We'll keep her here until after the meeting tomorrow night. Then we'll decide what to do," Néall said.

Gavin was listening at the chimney of the house where the men had Kalani. He flew to meet his sister, who by this time should have told Fionuir what was happening and be on her way, following the trail he'd marked.

Chapter Eleven

The town council meeting bustled with the usual pre-meeting gossip groups. Finally, the Mayor hit his gavel on the desk and called the meeting to order. In the crowd of townspeople were two strangers, one looking old and wise, the other, young and sullen. They sat at opposite ends of the gathering, both listening intently to the business at hand. Finally, the Mayor hit his gavel on the desk, bringing the meeting to a close. Rowan now knew the townspeople were innocent of all that was happening in the Fairy Forest. Néall now knew the townspeople had no idea what was going on in the Fairy Forest.

The two strangers stood and walked toward the door, reaching it at the same time. Their eyes met briefly. Rowan, ancient and wise, knew. Néall just wanted to get back to the house and deal with the *problem*.

Chapter Twelve

King Ailbhe welcomed the Elves to the council chamber. "Welcome, my brothers," Ailbhe took his chair at the head of the table. Rowan sat on one side of his King - King Fintan, on the other. Ailbhe turned to Rowan, "First order of business is to find out what news from the human council meeting you have for us?"

Rowan stood. "The townspeople made no mention of anything happening in our forest." He paused. "However, as I was leaving, I made eye contact with a man who had an air about him that left me unnerved. He was not a local. It seemed like he was in a hurry to leave. I believe he is one of the men the young fairies might have come upon."

Ailbhe stroked his beard. "What say you, my friend?" he turned to King Fintan.

Fintan stood. He had ruled over the Elf kingdom for 600 years. He was known as the White Ancient in many circles. His eyes were the colour of burning embers in a dying fire, black with flecks of crimson. "If it is not the locals infiltrating Fairy Forest, and if Rowan feels this man has something to do with it, we must find him. Where in the forest did Gavin and Gavina see these machines?"

"At the southern tip," Ailbhe replied.

"Ah, so that is why we have not seen them. We have stayed in the north as of late. I will ask Branigan to go and observe what is happening; they will not suspect a raven in the trees," Fintan said.

"I will have Olcán accompany him; a wolf in the forest will also go unnoticed," Ailbhe suggested. "Let them leave as quickly as possible. We will return here tomorrow night. Until then, you are my guests."

Chapter Thirteen

Fionuir did not like what she was hearing. These humans had overstepped their limits. Fairy Forest was the last safe refuge in Ireland for the Ancients who inhabited it. "Take me to these machines, Gavina. I will destroy them!"

Gavina studied the banshee. To the naked eye, everything about Fionuir was gray, except her eyes. The eyes blazed brightly through the mist shrouding her body - red, yellow, and orange flames melding together. Fionuir's eyes could strike fear into the bravest of men or creatures.

"I beg you first to go and free our friend Kalani. Gavin has left a trail for me to follow, and if I know him, if Gavin already knows where Kalani is, he will be backtracking now with the news of where these men have taken her."

Just as Gavina finished speaking, there was a knock on the door, but before Fionuir could answer it, Gavin burst inside.

"I know where she is! The beasts have tied her to a chair and sealed her lips! We must hurry!" Gavin was breathless. "They are not far from here," he added.

"I have a plan," Fionuir said. "Listen carefully." The banshee relayed her intentions to the twins before they set off to save Kalani.

Chapter Fourteen

Kalani concentrated her thoughts on Néall. He was the strongest of the three - physically and mentally. He would be the one she would have to break. *"Ye are trespassin' on land that does no' belong to you."*

Néall looked around for the owner of the voice. Conor and Liam had gone off to bed and Néall was sitting alone in the room with the girl. She appeared to be asleep as well, her mouth was taped shut.

"You'll no' be wantin' to be messin' with the inhabitants o' the forest."

Néall started to shake.

"I understand you don't believe in fairies and elves and such, but you would be wise ifn you remembered the stories you was tol' when you were a wee boy - remember, Néall?"

Néall bolted from his chair and came close to Kalani. She opened her eyes. He gazed deeply into them but drew back in fear from what he saw. They burned a flaming red, and in the fire of her soul, he saw creatures – fairies - torturing him in a murky world. "What are you?" he shouted at her.

"I am, as I have been born, as my people have been for thousands of years. We just wish to live in peace, undisturbed. Your kind promised us such."

"I never promised you anything!"

"Humans gave us that forest, and it is our last refuge. We will not let it go."

Néall turned at the sound of a knock on the door. "Who could that be at this time of night?" he grumbled. He pointed a finger at Kalani: "Not a word, girl," he ordered, despite the fact her mouth was taped shut.

Shivers ran down his spine at her silent reply, "I 'ave warned you; now it's up to you." A peal of light musical laughter followed the advice and the flames in her eyes danced unmercifully.

The knock came again. Néall answered the door, using his body to block the view into the room. He would get rid of whoever it was. His eyes opened in amazement - a petite boy and girl, alone at this time of night? On the boy's shoulder sat a hooded crow. The girl spoke first.

"Please, good sir, we are lost and hungry; could you give us a place to rest until morning's light so that we might then see better the path to our home?" Gavina's luminous, golden eyes pierced into Néall.

"I have no room here; you best be moving on. There's an old barn not far up the road," Néall added, feeling he must provide something for the unwanted visitors.

The children just stood there, smiling. The crow flew into the room before Néall could stop it.

~

"Uh, oh - too late! Welcome, my friends!"

Néall turned and saw the fire dancing mirthfully in Kalani's eyes. The children at the door began laughing.

"Where is that crow?" Néall shouted when he saw the woman swirling toward him. A high-pitched keen came out of her mouth, and wisps of gray surrounded him. He felt the breath forced from his lungs. "What are you?" he gasped, his eyes widening with terror.

"I think you know," Fionuir breathed. "You should never have taken so lightly your grandmother's stories of us."

Gavin and Gavina were busy untying Kalani. They turned toward the sound of a door opening. They smiled at the look on the faces of Conor and Liam. The two men stood mesmerized, their mouths gaping, their eyes round with fear at the scene before them.

"Let us be gone from here," Fionuir ordered. "We must take this man to King Ailbhe and make him tell the Fairy Council what is happening to our forest!"

The twins transformed into hawks. Kalani placed her hands in their claws and was flown out into the crispness of the early morning air. Fionuir gathered the unconscious Néall into her arms and floated through the door.

The last thing Conor and Liam heard was the wail of the banshee - like none they had ever heard - and they trembled with terror. The old tales had not prepared them for such a creature as they had just witnessed.

Chapter Fifteen

Killian was frustrated. Why didn't Néall answer his cell? Where was he? He was supposed to have reported in by now. Killian dialled again. This time he was rewarded with a voice, but not the one he was expecting. "Liam? Where's Néall?"

"He ain't here."

"Where is he? Put him on the phone!"

"The banshee ... she took him ... and the fairies ... they were fairies, they were, as sure as I'm standin' here ... they were fairies!"

"Stop your nonsense, man!" Killian fumed, his frustration at the foolishness of the men his foreman had hired building. "Put Néall on the phone!" Killian ordered.

"I tol' you; he's not here. The banshee took him; an evil one she was too! Her wail was not a comfort to us ... she took him up in her arms and left ... she and the children ... the hawks ... the fairies ... that's what they were ... fairies! You best be leavin' this project alone. You best not be messin' with the fairies. Me grandmother tol' me what happened last time our kind messed with the sprites!"

Killian shut his cell, not prepared to listen further to an obviously mad man. Killian got in his truck and sped off to the construction site. He could not afford to have anything go wrong with this project. His life depended on it.

Chapter Sixteen

Branigan and Olcán partially cleared the brush away from the machines.

"Looks like someone is planning to bulldoze our forest," Olcán growled.

"Sounds like a truck coming," Branigan declared. "Quick, cover the machines again; we don't want anyone to suspect we were here."

As Killian entered the clearing, he saw a wolf disappearing into the undergrowth. He didn't notice the raven in the tree above; he didn't discern that the wolf stopped, turned around, and was just sitting there, staring at him. Killian checked behind the brush to ensure the machines were still in one piece and then opened his cellphone. He was annoyed and tired of waiting on Néall and his crew to start the job they were hired to do. The phone was picked up on the fourth ring.

"Hey," a gruff voice answered. "Patrick, here."

"Killian, here, Patrick ... I'm goin' to be needin' a new crew ... don't know where Néall is ... those fools he had workin' for him kept mumblin' somethin' about fairies..."

Patrick burst into laughter: "Fairies, you say? Old people's tales!"

"Exactly. So, how soon can you round me up some men; I need to get this project on the go."

"Is tomorrow morning soon enough?" Patrick asked.

"Perfect. I'll meet you here in the morning at 7:00 ... thanks, man." Before hanging up, Killian gave Patrick directions to the construction site.

Killian took another look around the clearing, then returned to his truck. He rolled down his window. It was already hot, but the sky foretold a coming storm. What else could go wrong? He had promised these mansions would be well underway before the summer was out. As the engine chugged to a start, Killian noticed a raven circling at the edge of the wood. As he put the vehicle into drive, he heard the howling of a wolf.

Chapter Seventeen

The Fairy Council and the Elves gathered in King Ailbhe's chambers. Olcán and Branigan stood ready to give their report. Suddenly the door flew open, and Fionuir entered with her captive. She laid him on the table, stepped back, and bowed to the kings.

"A present for you, my lords," she grinned. "This man will be able to tell you what is happening in Fairy Forest."

"Greetings, Fionuir," Rowan stepped forward. "What of the children?"

"They are safe," she laughed, "and not likely to be heading out for adventures anytime soon. They are with Shanaye."

Rowan smiled. Everyone turned to Néall as he moaned and began to awaken.

~

Néall rubbed his eyes and sat up. He looked around in wonderment. "What the ... no ... you can't be ... yer not real..."

King Ailbhe smiled. "We are as real as you. We have lived in this forest for hundreds of years, and after the last human effort to invade us 99 years ago, an agreement was made to secure our forest and a ten-mile range of land beyond the river that flows around it. We have been made aware of an attempt to break this agreement. You are here to tell us what is going on."

Rowan stepped forward. "And do not try to blame it on the town's people; I was at the same meeting you were, remember?"

Néall shuddered as Rowan gazed deeply into his eyes. "Yes, I remember you; you were the old man blocking my way at the door."

King Fintan stepped closer to Néall. "It will be folly for humans to tamper with Fairy Forest. We do not wish to shed any blood, but we will protect what is ours; we have our ways of doing so." He smiled. Néall looked away and was silent.

Fionuir floated to Néall and ran her fingers down his cheeks, her nails leaving trickles of blood. "Leave the human alone with me and I shall extract all you need from him, my lords."

Néall shivered and shrank from the banshee's touch; her breath chilled him through.

"We thank you, Fionuir, for bringing him to us and for your generous offer, but I feel this man will tell us everything we need to know without too much persuasion. Here, let me help you off this table and offer you a chair," King Ailbhe proffered his hand to Néall. Néall looked from King Ailbhe to Fionuir, then took the King's hand, figuring he was the safer of his two options.

Once settled in the chair, Néall began to spill everything. He told how his boss, Killian, discovered the existence of this massive parcel of land and how he had approached some *business associates* with a plan to build a wooded community for the rich. Killian was adding a golf course resort all along the river, a couple hotels and fine-dining restaurants to accommodate themselves and their guests. His boss figured there was plenty of land in the woods, so lots would consist of two acres, and fallen trees would be used in a section of each of the houses. It would significantly enhance the economy of the area.

"So exactly what is your part in all this?" King Fintan interrupted.

"I'm just a labourer; my crew and I were to move the equipment in and Killian was arranging for the surveyors. We are supposed to begin this week."

Branigan stepped forward. "This man you speak of is meeting someone with a new crew at 7:00 tomorrow morning. Olcán and I overheard his phone conversation."

"Ah, so our time is short," King Ailbhe said. "We must make our plans quickly." He looked at Néall. "I thank you for your assistance; Fionuir will show you out."

Fionuir screeched in delight as she took Néall's arm and led him from the room, knowing what she was to do before releasing the human.

The elves and the fairies huddled together; three hours passed before they left the King's chambers. The hallways echoed with a mournful wailing. Rowan stopped at the room where Néall sat, ashen-faced, while Fionuir wrapped mistily around him. He entered and touched her on the shoulder. "I believe he has had enough; you must let him go if it is not yet his time."

She nodded and relinquished Néall to Rowan, not trusting herself to allow the man to live. Rowan took him up to the woods and watched as Néall stumbled off. Rowan felt sadness for the human, who was nothing more than a pawn in the scheme of things. If a man lived after being with Fionuir, they were never truly the same!

Chapter Eighteen

Killian arrived at the site early. His fingers tapped nervously on the steering wheel. He'd received a phone call from his investors last night, wondering what the holdup was. Killian assured them everything was all right.

He got out of the truck when he saw headlights bearing toward him. The air was chilled. The sky was blacker than night as the clouds raced by. Large droplets of rain began to fall. The trees in the forest swayed angrily, fighting with the elements.

As Killian greeted his new crew, the elves and the fairies were taking up their positions amongst the trees. A wolf howled. A raven landed on the roof of Killian's truck. The screeching of the banshee shattered the windshields of the vehicles sitting at the edge of Fairy Forest!

~

The workers staggered from their trucks as the glass splintered. The raven on the roof of Killian's vehicle swooped toward him. Killian ducked, but not soon enough. He lay flat on the ground, staring into the black eyes of the bird on his chest. His heart raced into overdrive when the bird spoke to him.

"You are trespassing on land that is not yours, Killian. I would suggest you take yourself and your men and leave this place!"

Killian started to swing his arms at the raven. Some of the workers ran up, trying to shoo the bird away, but it seemed as though an invisible wall surrounded the raven, for none of them could touch it. The raven clucked madly as it soared off, "Leave now! All of you!" it shouted as it flew into the forest.

There was a moment of shocked silence at the edge of the woods as the humans surveyed the damages. The trees groaned as the wind picked up, and the ebony clouds dipped into the upper branches. The river flowing by the forest danced over the shoreline. Killian finally stood and brushed the dust from his clothes.

"Okay, men, since you are all here, let's get started before the storm sets in; there's been enough time wasted," he shouted, despite what had just gone down.

The men hesitated. They did not like the looks of the sky or the woods. They disliked even more the eerie feeling that was left in their bones as the raven flew away.

"Move, you lazy lot, or I shall make sure none of you will have another construction job in fair Ireland ever again!" Killian was one of the biggest contractors in Ireland, and the men knew the power he wielded. They followed him into the forest. By the time they reached his side, he was straining to take the brush off the machines. "Give me a hand here. Those idiots I hired have tangled the brush in the machines. They better not be ruined!"

Suddenly a mist swirled out of the brush, accompanied by a high-pitched wailing. "You still dare to defy the laws that protect our forest, despite our warnings!" Fionuir landed in front of Killian. "Who has given you the rights to this land?"

As shaken as Killian was, he feared more the men from whom he had borrowed the money. They would see he didn't live to see another day if this project didn't move forward. "What are you?" he choked out the words.

"Your worst nightmare!"

"You cannot stop this progress; you are one against many!" Killian spouted with false courage.

"And you will not progress further with this business of yours!" King Ailbhe stepped out from the cover of the trees. Beside him was the most enormous wolf Killian had ever seen. On King Ailbhe's other side stood King Fintan with a raven on his shoulder. The earth began trembling - crevices formed around the machines. The trees parted and revealed the inhabitants of Fairy Forest - in full battle gear.

Killian turned to his men, ready to order them to action. What he saw were their backs. He felt a cold chill as Fionuir wrapped her arms around him. "Whoooo doooo you think you are?" she wailed into his ear. She turned his face so he could watch the massive machines disappear into the earth. "You are up against a force you will not conquer . We have powers beyond those you think you fear." She stepped back from him and he crumpled to the ground.

Rowan strode forward and knelt beside the broken Killian. "It is written in our laws that any human who dares to attempt to destroy our forest will meet with a horrible death. However, our Kings have conferred. They do not wish you harm, only that you be gone! I will take you to the place where I left your friend, Néall. There you will both be met by Orthanach and Sheelin. They will take you to the hidden lake and wipe your memories, as was done with those who previously left these woods; fear has sealed their memories this day."

Killian looked around him. He was alone in a world he had always denied existed. Whatever fate these creatures had in store for him would surely be better than the one Killian would face now that the project had failed. He allowed the fairies to lead him - not that he had a choice.

As Killian turned for a last look, he saw the two kings embracing. He saw the earth return to normal. He saw the broken branches that had covered his machines plant themselves in the ground and grow into tall trees. He saw the stone fence close in. He saw the fairies and the elves disappear into the woods. It was as if Fairy Forest was never touched!

Epilogue

Kalani and the twins, Gavin and Gavina, raced through the hallways of the fairy castle beneath the forest floor.

"Last one to the stone must move it!" Gavin shouted.

Kalani and Gavina giggled because they noticed who was standing at the end of the hallway - Rowan and Kalani's mother, Shanaye. The adults smiled, knowing exactly what the young fairies were up to. The girls were happy to be out of the way of trouble.

Rowan reached out and took hold of Gavin's arm as the young fairy skidded to a stop. "Where be you going, Gavin?"

Gavin swallowed hard, deciding not to admit anything that would get him into trouble. "Nowhere," he lied.

Rowan was wise enough not to push Gavin for a more honest answer. The young fairy had the potential to become a great leader eventually, and one never knew when there would be a need for one. If some humans had dared to defy the treaty now, it could happen again.

"I think it is time you began your serious lessons," Rowan grinned, looking toward Shanaye. "Kalani's mother will tend to her daughter and your sister; you are to come with me."

Gavin was confused when Rowan began his ascent up the stone stairs to the rock that covered the entrance into the forest. Kalani and Gavina were led in a different direction, making their way toward Shanaye's quarters.

Playtime was over for all three of the young fairies; they realized that soon they would no longer be classified as children. They were entering the adult world now.

Fifty years passed. Peace and quiet settled in Fairy Forest. The stone wall was taller now, not a treetop peeking over the uppermost level. The King ordered it so.

Gavin, who was now in charge of guard details, was wandering along the shore of the river, contemplating his upcoming marriage to Kalani. Rowan had taken him aside and said it was time to settle down and begin a family. Suddenly, Gavin heard a familiar sound. A roaring, not of the forest, coming from beyond the wall.

"Not again!" Gavin muttered as he turned and followed the trail back to the stone over the entrance to the underground fairy fortress.

Quickly, Gavin found Rowan in his quarters and told him what he heard. Rowan sighed. "We must tell the king," Rowan expressed. "We will not allow humans to get as far as they did before."

Within hours, a small army of fairies entered the trees, moving quickly to where Gavin heard the roar of an engine. When they arrived at the location, they listened to the commotion beyond the wall and felt the ground tremble as something smashed against the rocks.

As the fairies formed a line, they heard the keening of the banshee. Fionuir swept toward her friends in a shower of gray mist. The fairies began chanting and stamping their feet, joining the banshee's song.

On the other side of the stone fence, the earth opened up and swallowed the would-be intruders, then closed. It was as though the humans had never been there.

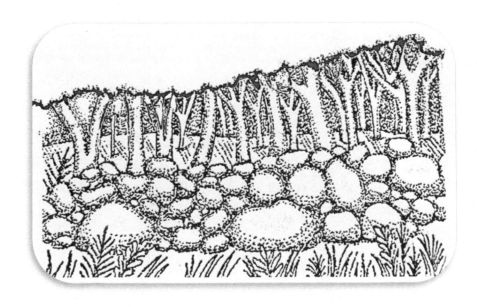

"You did well, Gavin," Rowan commented as the two walked side by side. In his heart, Rowan knew Gavin was being groomed to become King. And, Kalani was going to be the perfect queen to sit by his side.

Gavin nodded humbly. He was grateful for all the knowledge the fairy/elf continued to teach him. Childhood was left behind, but not all of it. Mischief still sparkled in Gavin's eyes, and would, without doubt, be passed on to his children when he and Kalani started their family.

At the stone entrance, Gavin hesitated and looked around the calm of the woods, breathing in the fragrance of peace. A peace he hoped to be able to maintain. Gavin laid a hand on Rowan's arm. "I shall be along shortly," he said.

Rowan nodded, knowing what Gavin was about to do. He watched the hawk take flight, flying over his future kingdom, ensuring all was well - for now. Rowan knew it would not be the last attempted intrusion, for as long as some humans were willing to destroy the sacred Fairy Forest for greed, the fairy world would never be truly safe.

Printed in Great Britain
by Amazon

68709034R00047